Branca Tani

New York

Clouds are made of water.
Water comes from
oceans, lakes, and rivers.

The sun heats the water.

Some water turns into gas.

The gas rises.

The gas gets cold
as it rises through the air.

The gas turns into
water drops in the sky.
Many tiny drops together
make a cloud.

The cloud floats
in the sky.
The cloud is moved
by the wind.

When the water drops
get too big, they fall
from the cloud.

The drops are called rain.

Do you like to play in the rain?

When it is cold,
snow falls from clouds.
Snow is frozen water.

It is fun to play in the snow.

We build a snowman
in the snow.

The wind blows the clouds away.

The rain stops.

The sun comes out.

Sometimes we can
see a rainbow after it rains.

Words to Know

cloud

rain

rainbow

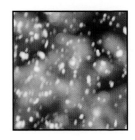

snow

snowman

sun